And Then Comes
SUMMER

With big-time love for Lizzie, Will, Wes, Jack, Roy, Coleman, Paloma, Olive, and Fox

T. B.

To Dad. Thank you for all the great summer memories.

J. K.

Text copyright © 2017 by Tom Brenner
Illustrations copyright © 2017 by Jaime Kim

First paperback edition 2021

Library of Congress Catalog Number 2017940755
ISBN 978-0-7636-6071-0 (hardcover)
ISBN 978-1-5362-1737-7 (paperback)

21 22 23 24 25 26 CCP 10 9 8 7 6 5 4 3 2 1

Printed in Shenzhen, Guangdong, China

This book was typeset in Agenda Medium.
The illustrations were done in acrylic paint with digital tools.

Candlewick Press
99 Dover Street
Somerville, Massachusetts 02144

visit us at www.candlewick.com

And Then Comes
SUMMER

TOM BRENNER

illustrated by **JAIME KIM**

CANDLEWICK PRESS

WHEN the days stretch out like a slow yawn,
and leaves and grasses sparkle with dew,
and the cheerful faces of Johnny-jump-ups jump up . . .

THEN throw on flip-flops and breathe the sweet air.

WHEN bumblebees bumble around in flowers,

and warblers flit from tree to tree,

and the air thrums with the sound of lawn mowers . . .

THEN pump up your bike tires,

dig out your helmet,

and raise your seat — my, how you've grown!

WHEN the last class project is finished,
and your cubby is cleaned of cookie crumbs and eraser bits,
and end-of-the-year hugs have been given . . .

THEN swap out backpacks and notebooks for pitchers and cups.

WHEN daylight pushes back bedtimes,
and crickets *crick-crick* in the evening air,
and bugs as big as thumbs bang against windows . . .

THEN play hide-and-seek until darkness wins.

WHEN stores unfurl the Stars and Stripes,

and flags wave from porches and cars,

and the whole town seems wrapped in bunting . . .

THEN dress up your bike and pedal to the parade.

WHEN bands march by — left, right, left, right —
and all manner of floats float past,
and Scouts and pioneers toss candy . . .

THEN grab your blanket and watch
the night explode in colorful sprays.

WHEN every day is like a Saturday,

and porches and lawns and sidewalks are playgrounds,

and a familiar jingle interrupts the game . . .

THEN race to be the first in line —

"Almond fudge, please!"

WHEN the dog days of summer roll around,
and it's so hot you're practically panting,
and not even the sprinklers provide relief . . .

THEN it's time to head to the lake.

Roll down the window and smell the hot, dry grass,

shout your favorite songs at birds swooping across fields,

and ask for the millionth time, "Are we there yet?"

LAKE
SUNNYSIDE

WHEN the familiar sign appears at last,
and the silver lake winks through the trees,
and old friends run to greet you . . .

THEN scramble out of the car,

dash down to the beach,

and swim till the sun is low and your lips are blue.

AND WHEN dinner is over and stories have been told,

and your fingers are sticky with marshmallow and chocolate,

and the fire burns down to glimmering coals . . .

THEN snuggle into your sleeping bag
and plan tomorrow's adventures.